Smoke Cat

Simon didn't actually see them do it – one minute they were there and the next they were gone – but the shadowy cats seemed to melt away into the ground, or fade like mist, into the flower-beds and shrubbery. The old lady stood alone, holding out her hands and looking up at the fence between the two gardens, "Blue! Blue, *please* come!"

Dare you try *another* Young Hippo Spooky?

The Screaming Demon Ghostie
Jean Chapman

The Kings' Castle
Ann Ruffell

Scarem's House
Malcolm Yorke

Five Young Hippo Magic stories to enjoy:

My Friend's a Gris-Quok!
Malorie Blackman

The Little Pet Dragon
Philippa Gregory

Broomstick Services
Ann Jungman

The Marmalade Pony
Linda Newbery

The Wishing Horse
Malcolm Yorke

Four Young Hippo Funnies to make you laugh!

Bod's Mum's Knickers
Peter Beere

Emily H and the Enormous Tarantula
Emily H and the Stranger in the Castle
Emily H Turns Detective
Kara May

LINDA NEWBERY

Smoke Cat

Illustrated by Anne Sharp

For Kate, Jonathan and Alexander

Scholastic Children's Books,
7-9 Pratt Street, London NW1 OAE, UK
a division of Scholastic Publications Ltd
London ~ New York ~ Toronto ~ Sydney ~ Auckland

Published in the UK by Scholastic Publications Ltd, 1995

ISBN 0 590 13438 8

Typeset by Backup... Design and Production, London
Printed by Cox & Wyman Ltd, Reading, Berks

10 9 8 7 6 5 4 3 2 1

Chapter 1

As soon as they saw 16 Parkside Terrace, Simon's mum and dad decided that this was the house for them.

"I've always wanted to live in an old house," Dad said. "A house other people have lived in. It's like an old pair of shoes, creaky and comfortable."

Simon wasn't sure. He thought of the

new houses they'd been to look at, with bright clean paintwork and fresh wallpaper. He would have liked to live in one of those. But Mum said, "They've

got no personality." She and Dad had the same ideas about houses, which was just as well. And this house was quite close to their old one, so Simon wouldn't have to change schools.

Dad said, "It's going to be a home, not just a house."

So they moved into the tall thin house that was nearly a hundred years old. It was made of red brick and it was sandwiched between others in a row like soldiers standing to attention. It had long narrow rooms with high ceilings, and there was a long narrow garden behind it. Simon's bedroom was at the back. He

liked the high ceiling and the old-fashioned fireplace, but he wasn't sure about all the other people who had lived there, who had slept in this room during its hundred years. He didn't know who they were, or what thoughts and memories and dreams they might have left behind.

It was the fireplaces that had really made up Mum's and Dad's minds. There were three – one in the main room downstairs, and one in each bedroom. Mum had always wanted a house with a real fireplace.

She stood in the downstairs room and said, "We can have a log fire sometimes. Won't that be lovely on a cold day?"

Simon thought it would, especially when Dad talked about roasting chestnuts in the ashes. But winter was a long way off. It was summer now, and the best thing about the house was the garden. It was much better than the bare fenced squares that went with the brand new houses, or the tidy patch they'd left behind at their council house. It was a real jungle of a garden, with tangly bits and hidden corners and shadowy secret places, and a high fence separating it from next door's garden.

Everything in the garden seemed eager to grow as big and as high and as lush as it could. The plants in the borders spilled over on to the grass as if they had lost

their balance. Ivy and honeysuckle clambered up the fence. Flowers whose names Simon didn't know stretched up their heads as if they wanted to get as near to the sun as they could. It was a garden for exploring, for crawling into the damp earthy shadowy places. There were snails and slugs and spiders and worms and ladybirds and caterpillars, and once Simon found a puff of scattered

feathers and a few small bones. There were thistles and nettles and brambles and plants with thick juicy stems, and berries that were not to be eaten. Simon knew he shouldn't eat them because they were black and glossy and delicious-looking, like poisonous berries in a fairy story.

"I shall have to do something with that garden," Mum said.

Simon wondered what she meant. The garden didn't need anything done to it. Everything in the garden knew what to do. The plants grew and the insects hatched and crawled and flew and nibbled.

Best of all, there was an apple tree. The blossom had finished and you could

already see the new little apples coming. There were helpful branches stretching out at right-angles and in just the right places, so that Simon could quite easily climb up to more than twice his own height above the ground, and wedge himself safely into a fork where the branches divided. From there, he could look down into the garden next door.

Chapter 2

Next door's garden was just as long and narrow, but less jungly. There were flowering shrubs and bushes planted all the way along its edges and in a big flower-bed that was right in the middle of the lawn, like an island. Someone looked after the garden very well, Simon could tell. An old lady was walking very slowly along the border, talking to herself. At least, that's what Simon thought she was doing at first, until he realized that she was talking to the plants. He clung tightly to the apple branch and listened.

"And how are you today, William?" the old lady asked a rose bush with peachy flowers. "My goodness, you are looking glossy. You always did enjoy the sunshine. Charlotte, my dear, you must stand up for yourself more – this forsythia will take up all the space if you let her. Gloria, how lovely to see you growing so tall and strong – you're going to be a fine lady one of these days. Frederick, you have a good rest now till next spring; you've earned it. Now, where's Blue..."

She was quite close to Simon. She wore a long brown cardigan and a tweedy skirt, and her grey hair was so thin that the pink of her scalp gleamed through it. She stretched out her hand to touch the leaves and petals of each plant as she spoke to it. Simon could see the papery skin of her hand, and the fingers, knobbly like twigs, and the big loose ring she wore on her left hand.

Simon thought she must be mad. He'd heard of people talking to plants – Mum did it sometimes, telling the Swiss cheese plant how clever it was to grow a new leaf, and according to the newspapers Prince Charles did it all the time. But this old lady gave them *names*. People's names. He was just wondering whether every plant in next-door's garden had a name, when the old lady turned round and saw him. She froze, with one hand stretched out to touch a tall white daisy in the island bed, and she stared at him.

Without meaning to let go of the branch he was clutching, Simon found himself slithering down from his perch and landing on the ground with a painful twist of his right ankle. He had grazed his hands and his knee on the apple-tree bark and he had landed hard on one elbow. He waited for a few moments, very

quietly, expecting the old lady's face to appear over the fence – she would probably tell him off for spying on her. Although he hadn't really been spying. All he had been doing was climbing a tree in his own garden.

"I don't like that lady next door," he told Mum when he went in for his tea. "She talks to herself."

Mum looked surprised. "Hazel? Oh, but she's really nice. We all talk to ourselves sometimes."

Simon wasn't sure about the old lady. He thought she might have told him off if he hadn't dropped down out of sight. She looked as if she might be strict. He didn't think Hazel was the right name for her at all. She ought to be called Mrs or Miss something.

Chapter 3

There was an alleyway at the end of the garden, which was the way Simon came in when he got home from school each day. One afternoon he let himself in at the back door to hear voices talking in the front room – Mum's and somebody else's. He went in, hoping there might be cake, and saw a lady of Mum's age or perhaps a bit older, with curly permed hair and bright red earrings. She was holding a mug of tea and she smelled of perfume. She smiled at him and said, "Hi, Simon," as if she had known him for ages. "I'm Hazel from next door."

That explained it! Mum had got this lady mixed up with the other one. He knew the old lady couldn't be called Hazel, and he couldn't imagine this one wandering round the garden talking to the plants. She looked too energetic, as if she might jump up from her chair any minute and start playing hide-and-seek; she was a jolly-looking person, unlike the older lady, who had looked quite sad.

"Hello," he said politely, really more interested in the cake. There *was* cake, a chocolate one with flake decoration.

"Does someone else live in your house?" he asked Hazel.

She laughed, as if she thought it was a funny thing to ask. "Just Bill. My husband. Have you seen him? You can't miss him – he's a great big bloke. Rugby-playing type."

And then it occurred to Simon that perhaps Hazel lived in the house on the other side – they had two next-door neighbours, after all. Perhaps he had been the one who made the mistake, not Mum. But when she left (after having a second piece of cake), Simon watched from the window, and saw her turn right and go up the path next door – the path to the house where the old lady lived.

"That wasn't the person I meant at all," he told Mum. "The one who was talking to herself."

Mum shrugged. "Perhaps she had someone to stay."

Simon didn't think the old lady was just staying – she had looked as if she lived there, knowing all the plants the way she did. But he didn't think about it any more that day, because he had a new computer game to play with and a drawing to do for school. He didn't think about it any more at all, until a few nights later when he woke up suddenly in the middle of the night to hear a voice calling, outside in the garden. The old lady's voice.

He couldn't hear *what* she was calling, but it went on and on, as if calling for someone who didn't come. He tried to go back to sleep, but the more he tried, the wider-awake he became. Eventually he got out of bed and pushed back the curtains.

It wasn't the middle of the night, as he had thought. It was just starting to get light; he could make out the dim shapes of trees, fences and flower-beds. And in the garden next door, the old lady,

stretching out her arms and calling.

"Charlotte!" He could hear now what she was saying. "Georgina, there's a good girl. Gladys, time to rest now. Geoffrey! Here's your place. Blue! Oh, Blue, won't you come?"

She was calling to the *plants* – Simon recognized the names. It was strange enough to be standing out in the garden at about three o'clock in the morning, but odder still to be calling out to *plants*.

And even more odd besides if she didn't actually live there.

She kept bending down to touch something, and as Simon's eyes adjusted to the first grey light he could see shadows moving around at her feet, rubbing against her legs – soft, fluid, furry shadows, like cats. Although they were shadowy, Simon could make out the

different colours: black cats, white cats, tabby cats, pied cats, marmalade cats. The old lady welcomed each one, stroking it, talking to it in a soft voice, until she was surrounded by a moving carpet of purring cats, weaving, twining, arching their backs to be stroked. And every few moments she would break off to stand upright and gaze around, and she would call, "Blue! Blue, won't you come?"

Simon didn't actually see them do it – one minute they were there and the next they were gone – but the shadowy cats seemed to melt away into the ground, or fade like mist, into the flower-beds and shrubbery. The old lady stood alone, holding out her hands and looking up at the fence between the two gardens. "Blue! Blue, please come!"

Simon looked where she was looking, towards the fence, and thought for a moment that he saw, balancing there but walking away, a large, smoke-grey, plume-tailed cat, faint as a shadow in the last few moments before the sun goes in.

"Blue!" The old lady's voice sounded despairing now. The cat disappeared into the hollies at the end of the garden, and the old lady turned towards the house.

Simon couldn't see her any more, and by the time he woke up later in the morning he thought he had dreamed the whole thing.

But next night the smoke cat came back by itself. It was a moonlit night, and when Simon was in his room getting ready for bed he glanced out of the window, just in case. There was no old lady, no voice calling, but on the fence Simon could see the smoke cat, treading softly towards the house, balancing on

delicate paws. The cat paused, looked down into next-door's garden, rubbed itself against a fence post as cats do, and then turned and walked off slowly, stopping to look back. Simon couldn't help thinking that it looked disappointed.

"Blue! Come back!" Simon had opened the window and was shouting out before he knew why. The cat paused and looked up at him for a moment, wafting its plume of a tail. Then it walked off, along the fence, towards the hollies, where it faded and vanished like smoke melting into the air. Watching the place where it had gone, Simon felt an ache of loneliness, although he didn't know why. There was nothing there at all to show that Blue had ever been.

Chapter 4

Two days later, Simon's mum had a dentist's appointment, and she told Simon that she wouldn't be in when he got back from school. "Hazel says you can go round to her house till I get home," she told him, "and she'll get you some tea."

Hazel seemed to be the sort of person who liked sticky cakes for tea, so Simon

didn't mind that at all. It was hot and sunny on Thursday afternoon, and Hazel came in from weeding the back garden when he arrived. She stopped to fetch Coke and jam doughnuts from the kitchen (Simon wasn't disappointed) and then they both went outside.

The garden looked a bit messier than Simon remembered it, although there was a bucket and a big pile of pulled weeds where Hazel had been working. He looked round, thinking that he knew some of these plants by name: Charlotte, Frederick, Gloria, William. But it would have sounded silly to say so. He wondered whether Hazel knew their names too.

"Did you plant all these flowers?" he asked her.

Hazel laughed. "Goodness, no." She snipped a dead flower from one of William's branches. "It takes a long time to get a garden looking like this. I just tidy it up now and then. No, my mother did most of the planting."

That explained it, although he still didn't know why Hazel hadn't told him her mother lived there, when he'd asked her the other day. Perhaps she was upstairs having a lie down. Old people did that, sometimes.

"Where is she?" he asked.

Hazel looked surprised. "My mum? Oh, she's dead now. She died two years ago."

Simon nearly said, "But she can't have done. I've seen her," until he realized that this was impossible; and besides, Hazel ought to know. He didn't *know* what to

say. He looked towards the house as if Hazel's mother might come out of the shadows. But there was no one there.

"Does – I mean did – your mother like cats?" he asked Hazel.

Hazel gave him a look of astonishment. "Yes! She was dotty about them. How did you guess?"

"Er – I just wondered." Simon was beginning to feel a bit peculiar. He eyed the third doughnut which was sitting by itself on the plate and wondered whether Hazel would mind if he had it. It would be a relief to eat another doughnut.

Doughnuts were solid and real, unlike old ladies who called to their cats in the middle of the night.

"Yes, she had dozens of cats over the years," Hazel said, looking towards Charlotte and not noticing how longingly

Simon was staring at the doughnut. "Four or five at a time. Of course they died sometimes, usually of old age. Whenever that happened she'd go to the garden centre and buy a new shrub and plant it, in memory – so nearly every plant in the garden's got a cat attached to it, if you see what I mean." Hazel gave a little laugh, as if she thought Simon might find this silly. "She even gave the plants names. Gloria, I remember... Frederick... I can't remember half of them now."

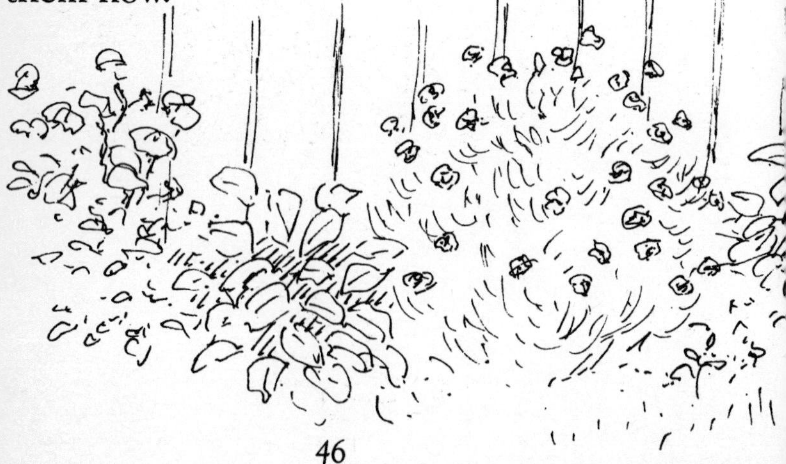

Simon wondered what she would say if he added, "Well, there's Charlotte, and there's Geoffrey..." But he didn't say anything. He was wondering about Blue. Why wouldn't Blue come into the garden, like the others? What did Blue want?

"She had a lovely cat just before she died," Hazel said. "A long-haired fluffy cat – grey, or more like blue-grey. She called him Blue."

"Yes, I know. I've seen him." This time the words were out of Simon's mouth before he could stop them.

Hazel stared at him.

"No, you can't have done," she said. "Blue died, a few weeks after Mum did. He wasn't very old. I don't know if a cat can pine, but I'm sure Blue pined for her." She frowned. "Maybe there's another cat around that looks a bit like Blue. But he was an unusual cat, not the sort you see very often."

No, it was definitely Blue. Simon didn't say it, but he thought it. And then, like a whisper, he saw the smoke cat, a shadowy, furry shape creeping out from the deep shade of the hollies and wafting along the fence like a curl of smoke.

"There he is!" Simon shouted, before he could stop himself.

Hazel whipped round and looked straight at Blue, who paused, one paw lifted, and stared back. Then Hazel turned back to Simon, half-smiling, half-puzzled.

"There's nothing there. You're having a game with me."

"I'm not! He *is* there! Look!"

Just as before, Blue walked along the fence, hesitated as if about to jump down into the garden and then stopped. His mouth opened in a silent miaow and he curled himself around on the spot and

turned away. Just as before, Simon had the sense that Blue was disappointed. With a lash of his plume tail, Blue walked carefully along the fence towards the deep shade of the hollies. Simon's eyes followed the blurry shape until he was unsure whether it had ever been there. Hazel had got tired of the joke she thought he was playing, and had gone back to her weeding, not noticing.

Just then Mum arrived from the dentist's, with her mouth all lopsided from the injection she'd had. "Come on, Shimon," she said, keeping her mouth shut as tight as a ventriloquist's. "It'sh time to go home. Thanksh for having him, Hashel."

Indoors, Simon ran up to his room and looked out of the window, thinking about the things Hazel had said. It was obvious

that she hadn't seen or heard the old lady, nor did she see the smoke cat on the fence. As far as he could tell, he was the only person who saw them. It gave him the odd feeling that he was supposed to do something about it. Blue wanted something, and Simon sensed he was the only person who could try to guess what it was.

Chapter 5

In the days and nights that followed, the old lady and the cat came back several times. There was no pattern to it. Sometimes, when he heard the old lady calling, it would be the middle of the night. Sometimes it would be broad sunlight, and she would be standing there in the garden for anyone to see, if only anyone else *could* see. Once, when Simon was watching from the apple tree, Hazel's husband Bill walked within inches of her without noticing.

Sometimes the old lady would be on her own, talking to her plants; sometimes she would be surrounded by her purring carpet of cats. But always she would be calling for Blue, and always Blue would turn away, disappointed. The old lady and Blue became so much a part of Simon's thoughts that he didn't know whether he dreamed them or really saw them. He only knew that he had to help them in some way – that he was the only person who *could*.

One afternoon, in desperation, he chased Blue right down the garden. It was useless; he should have known it would be. All that happened was that Blue vanished like a wisp of smoke into the evergreen depths of the hollies, and Simon plunged through the bushes on his own side of the fence, shouting, "Blue! Blue! Wait!" Even while he was shouting

he knew that the smoke cat wouldn't wait; and he didn't even know what he would have done if somehow he had caught Blue. You can't catch and keep a ghost cat; you can't make it stay. At the end of the chase Simon found himself standing hopelessly in the thickest and thorniest bushes, with his face scratched, his sweatshirt snagged and his knees and hands grazed and stung. Blue was nowhere to be seen.

Mum stared at him when he went indoors. "What on earth have you been doing?" She didn't sound too pleased. "You look as if you've been dragged through a hedge backwards."

Forwards rather than backwards, but otherwise fairly true, Simon thought. It was too difficult to explain; who would believe him? "Just playing in the garden," he said off-handedly.

"Well, I wish you'd put something old on first," Mum said, still a bit cross. "That sweatshirt used to be quite smart." She was collecting her things together: purse, bag, cheque-book. "Do you want to come and help me choose a present for Hazel? It's her birthday on Sunday and she's invited us round."

"Where are you going to get it?" Simon asked suspiciously. He didn't fancy trailing round perfume counters or looking at lacy scarves.

"I thought I'd go to the garden centre," Mum said. "Hazel's so keen on gardening – always out there digging and planting."

Simon wasn't sure why he agreed to go – garden centres weren't the most exciting places – but nevertheless he did. The garden centre was a huge place, with garden chairs and tools inside, and long avenues outside stretching into the distance, labelled *Climbers* or *Herbaceous Perennials*.

Mum started looking at hanging baskets bursting with pink geraniums and purple petunias, but Simon's attention was caught by the rows of bigger plants, all carefully looked after in their peaty-smelling containers, supported by sticks and labelled with their names. He looked at some, but they were in Latin and didn't

mean much to him. He found himself thinking, There's a Charlotte, and, That rose over there's a bit like William. And then it occurred to him. Blue didn't *have* a plant like the other cats, because the old lady had died first and hadn't been able to get him one. All the other cats came home to their own plant, but Blue always went away disappointed.

Here's my chance! Simon thought. I'll have to make Mum buy a Blue plant.

He walked along the rows, looking for a plant that would suit the smoke cat. There was row after row of yellow-flowered shrubs, pink-flowered climbers, scarlet perennials, some plants with no flowers at all. Nothing that would do. His spirits sank with dismay. If he didn't find the right plant here, where could he find it?

And then, turning a corner, he saw it at the end of a row ahead of him. It was so obviously the right plant for Blue that it seemed to call out to him. It had clusters of flowers like puffs of blue smoke, floating in a haze against darker leaves. He bent down as if greeting it, stroked the leaves, and then turned over

the label and read it. *Ceanothus Cerulea.* A smoke plant for the smoke cat.

He tracked down Mum, who was looking at some garish marigolds, and said, "I've found it! Just what Hazel wants."

"I was thinking perhaps a nice planted arrangement..."

"No. This is what she wants!" Simon dragged her by the hand to where *Ceanothus Cerulea* was waiting. Mum was still looking back longingly at the brassy marigolds, but in the end she gave in and got out her cheque-book and Simon carried *Ceanothus Cerulea* to the counter inside.

Chapter 6

Next day, at Hazel's, Simon couldn't wait until after the birthday tea for *Ceanothus Cerulea* to be planted. The garden table was loaded with all sorts of delicious things, and Hazel's husband Bill had made her a special cake with candles on it. Usually Simon's stomach would have started gurgling with delight, but not today – not yet. Blue's plant must come first.

"But I haven't decided where to put it yet," Hazel said, laughing. She was wearing new earrings and a new striped T-shirt and looked younger, not older, than she had done yesterday.

"I'll help you," Simon said. He dragged her towards the island bed and pointed. "Look, there. Just between Charlotte and Gloria. Blue's going to get quite big, so he'll need a bit of space."

Hazel stared at him. "Blue?"

"Yes. *You know.*" He looked at Hazel hard, meaning *Don't say anything to Mum and Dad – they won't understand.* He wasn't sure whether Hazel understood, but she looked at him oddly for a bit longer, then nodded and went and fetched a spade and a bag of bedding

compost. Simon helped with some of the digging – the ground was hard and dry – and when the hole was big enough,

Hazel's expert fingers arranged the earth around *Ceanothus Cerulea*'s roots as if she were tucking it into bed. Soon the new plant was firmly in its place, looking quite at home – cosily nestling between its two larger neighbours, but with plenty of room to grow.

"Now can we have our tea?" Simon's dad said, looking hungrily at the iced cake. "I had no idea you were so keen on gardening, Simon. There's plenty for you to do to our own jungle, if you want to get cracking. There's weeding and mowing and pruning and—"

"Not gardening," Simon said hastily. "Just this one plant."

He had done the best he could, but now he wanted to know that it had worked. When Hazel had blown out her forty candles and the cake had been cut and most of it eaten, Simon and his

parents went home. A little later, when the daylight started to fade, Simon went up to his room and looked out.

Nothing was happening. The garden table was still there, four garden chairs around it; Hazel's spade and compost-bag were beside the island bed where she had left them. There was no old lady, no smoke cat.

"Oh, come on, Blue!" Simon whispered, his mouth against the window. "I haven't gone to all this trouble for *nothing* – you *must* come now..."

Obstinately, the shadows refused to quiver into life and resolve themselves into the shape of a smoke cat. There was just a bare fence, and the hollies.

And then he heard, very faintly, "Charlotte, come along! William, there's a good boy! Gloria, where have you been?"

He craned his neck as far as he could. There she was, Hazel's mother, in her baggy cardigan and her droopy skirt, walking out from the patio into the dusk. The dim light streamed with furry shapes, surging, leaping down on to the grass, twining, tails high. The old lady walked as far as the island bed and then she saw *Ceanothus Cerulea.* She paused, and stretched out a hand to touch it as if she wasn't sure it was really there. Simon hardly dared breathe. The shadows by the hollies quivered and shook themselves into the shadowy shape of a cat. Blue. He sat, paused, and then trotted along the fence with his plume tail held high.

"Blue! Blue, come down!" The old lady's voice was hopeful, not despairing. Blue hesitated, opened his wide mouth once in a silent miaow, and then bounded down into the garden, where his shadowy shape merged with the other cats. Hazel's mother bent down to stroke him, and then the smoke cat took one joyful leap and landed lightly on her shoulders, twining himself around her ears. Just for a second, Simon thought the old lady looked up towards his window, and he saw her fleeting smile. The whole garden was filled with purring.

And then Simon blinked, and there was nothing there at all; just the silent gardens, and a rising moon.

The End